The Christmas Humbugs

By
Colleen Monroe

Illustrated by
Michael Glenn Monroe

Sleeping Bear Press

Sleeping Bear Press
310 North Main Street
P.O. Box 20
Chelsea, MI 48118
www.sleepingbearpress.com
1-800-487-2323
Printed and bound in Canada.

10 9 8 7 6 5 4 3 2

Library of Congress Cataloging-in-Publication Data
Monroe, Colleen.
The Christmas Humbugs / written by Colleen Monroe ; illustrated by Michael Glenn Monroe.
p. cm.
Summary: Magical creatures known as the Humbugs do mischievous
things to test a household's Christmas spirit.
ISBN 1-58536-108-9
[1. Christmas—Fiction. 2. Stories in rhyme.] I. Monroe,
Michael Glenn, ill. II. Title.
PZ8.3.M758Ch 2002
[E]—dc21

2002012751

To Natalie, Matthew, and John for your true spirits
and to Mike who has lived this dream for over 20 years.

—Colleen Monroe

To my mother, who helped me start this story so long ago...
and to my wife Colleen who helped me finish it.

—Mike Monroe

Legend has it long ago, in a land not far away,

magical creatures came to life one snowy winter day.

Nobody knows how they came to be,

or perhaps they will not say,

but every Christmas season

they come out to play.

Some say they're called the Humbugs

because they're itty-bitty things,

with messy hair, a big red nose, and shiny little wings.

On the ends of their antennae

dangle jingling bells of gold,

and there's a smell about them

like a fruitcake that is old.

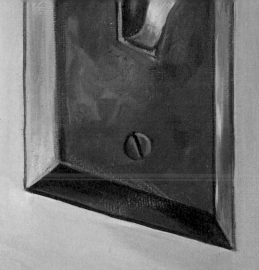

Each and every year

they pick a cheerful house,

and through the locks they sneak inside

as quiet as a mouse.

They tiptoe up and down the halls

in stockings red and white,

to do their little playful tricks

while you're tucked in bed at night.

They come in full of mischief

to play naughty little games,

like ripping holes in stockings

and breaking candy canes.

They aren't trying to be nasty,

in fact the opposite is true,

they're testing Christmas Spirit

and how strong it is in you.

Their favorite food is cookies

and they stop to eat a treat,

so on the plate for Santa

there is nothing left to eat.

Drinking Santa's ice cold milk

isn't as easy as you think,

if the Humbugs are not careful

they might fall into the drink.

The Humbugs love the Christmas lights,

they like the way they glow.

They twirl and hang and swing on them,

like a humbug rodeo.

Oh, what fun the Humbugs have

with a game of hide-and-seek,

sneaking through the Christmas tree,

from behind the bulbs they peek.

They like the shiny Christmas bulbs,

in every shape and size,

it's really fun to play with them

and win a tiny prize.

They use the toy tin soldiers

as their little bowling pins,

only to send them flying

when they give the bulbs a spin.

Underneath the Christmas tree,

where packages abound,

they cut off all the nametags

and then switch them all around.

They want to know what's in each gift,

so they make a tiny tear,

but before you can say "Bah Humbug,"

there is paper everywhere.

To: Heather
From: your favorite Artist

Bouncing up the Christmas tree

the little tricksters go,

and when they reach the tippy-top,

they give the star a throw.

But if they are not careful

as they set the bright star sailing,

they just might make an unplanned trip

with legs and wings a-flailing.

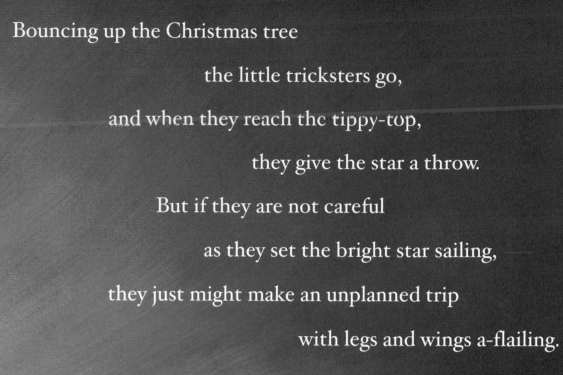
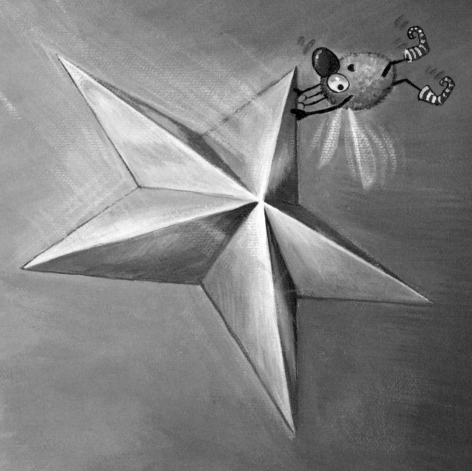

While they're in the Christmas tree,

on each branch they jump and hop,

working hard to shake it

and make all the needles drop.

They think themselves quite funny

as they stick them in their hair,

not thinking of the sticky sap

until they've stuck them everywhere.

They then turn back to see
all the damage they have done,
but what they see is that they haven't
bothered anyone.

The star is placed up on the tree,
the lights are all put back,
there's the smell of fresh-baked cookies
cooling on the baker's rack.
Someone swept the broken bulbs,
the candy canes are all replaced,
the spirit of Christmas is everywhere
and lives strong within this place.

Christmas spirit is not about the gifts,

the wrappings, or the bows,

Christmas spirit is the joy, the laughter,

the loving way it shows.

The Humbugs decide it's time to leave,

their mischievous work is done,

they've tested Christmas spirit

and they've had a little fun.

The Humbugs know true spirit

isn't bothered by their tricks,

the tiny pranks they play

take just a little time to fix.

So off they fly to another house,

back here they'll never come,

because of all the Christmas spirit

that they found in everyone.

As they fly into the night,

one last trick they can't resist,

they take apart the snowman,

whom earlier they had missed.

Oh, well it is their nature

and it shouldn't bring much sorrow,

it will be fun to fix him up

and play outside tomorrow.

COLLEEN MONROE is a graduate of the University of Michigan and spent many years in advertising before becoming a full-time mother. Her first book was the popular *A Wish to be a Christmas Tree*, also painted by her husband Michael.

Award-winning wildlife artist **MICHAEL GLENN MONROE** began his career at a very young age. A self-taught painter, Michael spends his time meticulously honing his craft, often teaching himself many new and unique techniques to add to his paintings.

Mike is thrilled to see *The Christmas Humbugs* finally in print, as he created the characters in high school over 20 years ago. *Humbugs*, like his titles *Buzzy the bumblebee* and *Foursome the Spider*, shares Mike's sense of humor by featuring delightful creatures who show readers how to follow their hearts.

Michael began his publishing career with Sleeping Bear Press in 1999 when both *Buzzy* and *M is for Mitten: A Michigan Alphabet* were released. His knowledge and experience with landscapes and wildlife were a perfect match for *Mitten* as well as subsequent state alphabet titles (*S is for Sunshine: A Florida Alphabet* and *L is for Last Frontier: An Alaska Alphabet*).

Michael and Colleen share a home in Brighton, Michigan with their three children, twins Matthew and Natalie and little John, born in May 2001.

By Colleen Monroe
Illustrated by Michael Glenn Monroe

Also by Colleen Monroe and
Michael Glenn Monroe:
A Wish to be a Christmas Tree

A little squirrel was wandering by
and stopped to hear the big tree cry.
"Take heart my friend and don't you fear,
to many of us you are so dear."